P9-DWW-430

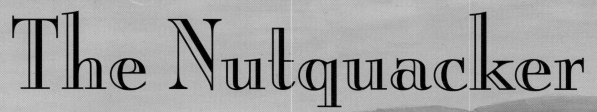

The Nutquacker

written and illustrated by
MARY JANE AUCH

Holiday House / New York

CLARA was a farm duck
and this was her first winter.
One morning, she noticed the older
farm animals whispering together.

"Coooool it!" mooed the cow
when Clara came near.

"I won't say-hay-hay-ay another
word," whinnied the horse.

"Just go ba-a-a-ack to your pond,"
the sheep bleated to Clara. "We have
pla-a-a-ans to make."

Over the next few days, Clara tried
to eavesdrop. She didn't hear much,
but one word came up over and over.
"I know your secret!" Clara told the
horse. "It's Christmas!"
The horse only smiled.

"So . . . what exactly is Christmas?" Clara asked. "Will you show me?"

"Try to be pay-hay-hay-hatient," whinnied the horse. "You'll find out."

Clara wasn't very good at being patient. "I can't wait. Will you take me to Christmas, Horse?"

"I never travel far from my own neigh-neigh-neighborhood," whinnied the horse. "Just stay here on the farm and way-hay-hay-hait."

"But I want to go now!" Clara insisted. "How about you, Cow? Will you help me find Christmas?"

"No, Christmas will come sooooon enough," mooed the cow. "Besides, all that moooooving around might turn my milk to milkshakes."

"What about you, Sheep?" asked Clara. "Won't you join me in a wild and woolly search for Christmas?"

"This is a ba-a-a-a-ad time to go wandering off," bleated the sheep. "I ca-a-a-a-an't leave right now."

"You'd rather stand around doing nothing?
You're all crazy!" quacked Clara.
"We're not cray-hay-hay-hazy," whinnied the horse.
"You're the looooony one," mooed the cow.
"You're a nutty duck, a real
nutqu-a-a-acker!" bleated the sheep.

"Nutquacker! Nutquacker!" teased the pig,
who was usually the butt of jokes himself.
"Every one of you is a stick-in-the-mud,"
mumbled Clara. "I'll go find Christmas all alone."
As she set off, it began to snow.

It snowed harder as Clara trudged along. She brushed the snowflakes from her beak and kept waddling until she came to a tall mountain. "I'll be able to see the whole world from the top of that mountain," she said. "That's how I'll find Christmas."

Clara struggled until she reached the very top. "I made it!" she cried.

A giant monster with huge eyes waited in the field ahead of her.

"Christmas must be hidden behind those trees in the distance. I can't turn back just because a giant monster with huge eyes is blocking my path. I may be small, but I'm smart. I'll find a way to get by him."

Clara slid down the other side of the mountain, gathered up her courage, and walked right up to the monster. "Watch out, Monster," she quacked. "I might look like an ordinary duck, but if you try to hurt me, I'll make you disappear."

The monster didn't move an inch. He didn't even blink.

Clara smiled. "Wise choice, Monster. You don't touch me. I don't zap you."

Clara circled the monster, just to prove how brave she was. Then she waddled on across the field, pleased with her cleverness.

But it wasn't long before a new danger loomed ahead.

"A large animal with sharp horns," Clara quacked. "No problem. If I could fool a giant monster with huge eyes, a large animal with sharp horns should be easy to trick." As she drew closer, Clara yelled, "Back off, large animal!"

Before Clara could say another word, the animal
ran away. "I'm getting good at this," Clara said,
"but I'm tired, hungry, and cold and I still haven't
found Christmas."

Clara hadn't traveled far before something else
blocked her path.

"A small creature with soft fur," Clara quacked. "Piece of cake. If I could outwit a giant monster with huge eyes and a large animal with sharp horns, a small creature with soft fur won't stop me from finding Christmas. Be careful, small creature!" Clara drew closer.

The creature didn't run away.

"I may look like an ordinary duck," Clara quacked, "but I'm powerful. If you touch even as much as one of my feathers, I'll turn you into a pile of dust."

The creature didn't move a hair.
"Way to go," Clara said, as she waddled past him.
"You don't hurt me. I don't pulverize you."

Suddenly, Clara felt a sharp pain in the tail feathers. She whirled around.

"I'm touching feathers here," said the creature. "Do I look like a pile of dust to you?"

"Don't talk with your mouth full," Clara said, thinking fast. "I've stopped a giant monster with huge eyes. I've scared off a large animal with sharp horns. No small creature can stand in my way."

The creature's eyes narrowed. "Then I won't stand.
I'll pounce!"

Just as the creature lunged for Clara, the feathers tickled
his nose. He started to sneeze, giving Clara the chance she
needed to escape. She waddled for dear life through the
falling darkness, listening to the sneezing fit behind her.

But Clara knew that when the sneezing stopped,
the creature would come after her.

Finally, Clara had to stop to catch her breath. She hid under some low-hanging branches, hoping the creature wouldn't discover her. "Why did I ever leave the farm and my friends?" she whimpered. "I'd give anything to be with them now. But I've come so far, I don't know how to find my way back."

Then she noticed a light cutting through the
darkness ahead. Was it shelter or a new danger?
Though she knew it was risky, Clara left the protection
of her hiding place. "That light is my only hope,"
she gasped. She waddled toward it at full speed.

Clara heard the creature closing in behind her. She gathered her last bit of strength and plunged through the drifting snow.

Clara burst through a door
and found herself in a magical
but familiar place.

All of her farm friends were there. "I'm home!"
she cried. "I'm so glad to see you. I must have been
walking in a big circle the whole time."

"Clara's ba-a-a-ack!" bleated the sheep.

"Just in time to celebray-hay-hay-ate Christmas!"
whinnied the horse.

"With lots of delicious foooood!" mooed the cow.
The pigs didn't say anything. They were too busy eating.

"We couldn't tell you we were
pla-a-a-a-anning a surprise Christmas
party," bleated the sheep. "We made you
a special present. It's a nutqua-a-a-a-acker."

"Just for yooooou,"
mooed the cows.
Clara hugged the nutquacker.
"I love it. I'm sorry I was so
mean before."
From then on, the animals
danced the night away.

"So Christmas is treats
and dancing and getting
presents?" asked Clara.

"Christmas is giving, tooooo!"
mooed the cows.

"Tha-a-a-t's not all," bleated
the sheep. "Christmas is being with
the ones who love you."

As the party
drew to a close,
Clara looked around
at all of her friends.
She was already
thinking of Christmas
gifts to make for
them next year.

For Kera,
Welcome
to the Auch
family

Book design by Sylvia Frezzolini Severance

Library of Congress Cataloging-in-Publication Data

Auch, Mary Jane.
The nutquacker / written and
illustrated by Mary Jane Auch–1st ed.
p.   cm.
Summary: Clara the duck is so impatient to discover the farm animals' secret
of Christmas that she puts herself in danger and almost misses the party.
ISBN 0-8234-1524-4
[1. Ducks—Fiction. 2. Domestic animals—Fiction.
3. Christmas—Fiction.]   I. Title   PZ7.A898Nu   1999
[E]-dc21   99–18347   CIP

This book belongs to:

_____

Library and Archives Canada Cataloguing in Publication

Bellegris, Agnes, 1970-
    Days to treasure : a book of seasons / written by Agnes Bellegris ; illustrated by
Katerina Mertikas.

Poems.
ISBN 978-0-9810529-1-5

    1. Seasons--Juvenile poetry. I. Mertikas, Katerina, 1957- II. Title.

PS8603.E455D39 2009   jC811'.6   C2009-902239-7

Cover and book design by Lisa Papathanasakis

Printed in China

To AM and the chumplings.
And to LP – I couldn't have done it without you.
Agnes Bellegris

The art in this book is dedicated to: my daughters Loukia
and Gina who encouraged me to illustrate a book, my grandchildren
who love to look at my art, my husband Dimitry, my kind parents
Georgina and Antonios Patrinos and my supportive brother Harry.
Katerina Mertikas

On today's walk to school
This third week of September
The air is crisp.
A chill has found its way on the breeze.

A cool wind is rising
Autumn is arriving.

Children in their classroom

Glance wistfully out the window,

Pensively pondering summer long-gone,

Anxiously anticipating

Halloween adventures

fast approaching.

Clocks shift. It's 3:20.

The final bell rings
Signalling the end
Of this day's learning.

Bidding goodbye
Children exit the building
Glancing above and below
At leaves so many and plenty
that are crimson, amber and gold.

They're crushed with a crunch
And squashed with a squash
By little feet
that pound the ground.

Fall's early night
Puts pleasant sunshine to sleep
Until the next day's dawning.
The night sky **glows gently**
A purply-grey by the light
Of the harvest moon rising.

Halloween finally!

Trick or treat! Children holler

With contagious excitement

Taking hold

Of both young and old.

Winter creeps in
With arctic weather's
Cold and snow.
Dress warmly dear children
The fun is about to begin.

Hang on to your toboggans!
From the top of a snow-covered hill
Look out below!

Festive, shining lights
Throughout the long, dark nights
Make children glee with anticipation
Of colourful gifts and tasty treats.
And who can forget the new start to the year –
Another occasion for celebration.

A blanket of sparkly, shimmery snow

On a wonderful winter's day

That's comfortably cold

Is an invitation for cooperation,

To build a new friend,

To play with and pretend –

But who will melt away

With winter's end.

How about hockey?
A traditional winter sport
of which we're so fond.
It takes place on a frozen pond
and involves teamwork and aim.
Sticks hit and slap
a sturdy black puck.
You're here to join us,
Oh, what good luck!
We need one more player
To make the teams fair.

Winter's sun-drenched days
Seem inviting from indoors
But outside is bitter,
BONE-CHILLING COLD.
It's hard to believe
Spring will soon unfold.

Snowfall does wane
And turns to rain
As temperatures rise
To warm the air.
The thaw has come.
Children stroll to school
Donning raincoats and rubber boots
Looking so cute
Splash-spattering in puddles
Clutching umbrellas above their heads.

This Sunday's amicable afternoon
In a friendly school field
Brings with it
A *zealous wind*
That's wholehearted,
Whisking cotton ball clouds
Through a blue radiant sky
Creating a congregation –
An energetic creation
Of kites that can fly
Ever so high.

Smell spring's fresh beginnings.
Cherry blossom blooms
Softly declare
Scented greetings,
And welcome tidings
For eleven children
Who frisk and frolic in the park,
With carefree laughter
That sounds like a melody in the air.

The school year's end

Marks the start of summer fun

With longer days of amusement

In the sun.

Riding bicycles, scooters and blades

In the neighbourhood

Is a merry adventure for everyone.

When it's time to rest

A cool, refreshing Neapolitan cone

Is nothing less

Than simply the BEST!

A hot afternoon takes children away
For a day at the beach.
It's a marvellous outing
Of splashing and laughing
And regal sand castle constructing
At the water's wet, wave-washing shore…

Maybe tomorrow they can do this once more.

It's hard to believe
In the midst of one season
Another will greet us.

But changing weather
Brings gentle reminders
Of times filled with pleasure.
Year after year
Seasons come packaged
With days to treasure.